First published in *Fairy Tales* 2000 by Walker Books Ltd
87 Vauxhall Walk, London SE11 5HJ

This edition published 2010

2 4 6 8 10 9 7 5 3 1

This book has been typeset in Palatino

Printed in China

British Library Cataloguing in Publication Data:
a catalogue record for this book is available from the British Library

ISBN 978-1-4063-2981-0

www.walker.co.uk

THIS WALKER BOOK
BELONGS TO:

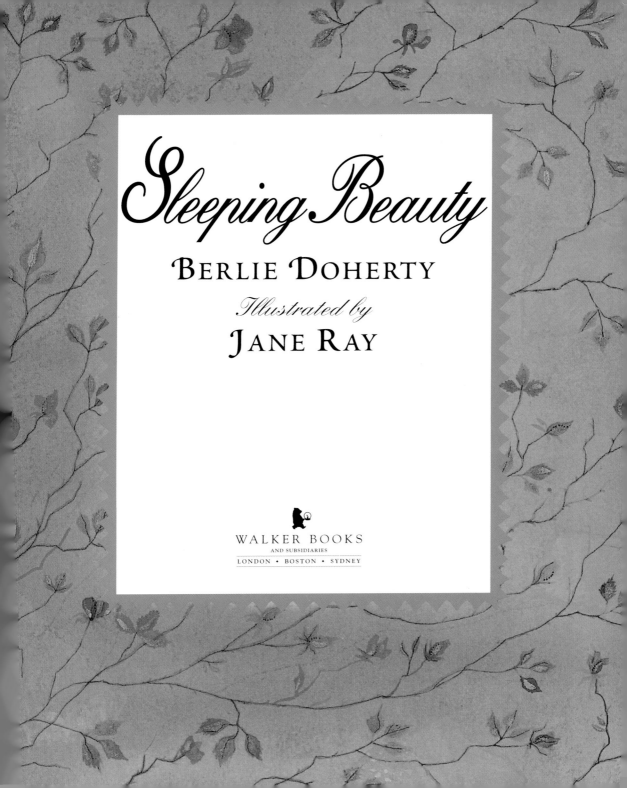

Sleeping Beauty

BERLIE DOHERTY

Illustrated by

JANE RAY

WALKER BOOKS
AND SUBSIDIARIES
LONDON · BOSTON · SYDNEY

One day a queen was walking alone in her beautiful rose garden. She had everything she could wish for except the thing she wanted most. As she passed a briar rose bush she heard a pitiful fluttering and saw a golden bird trapped in its branches. "Oh, poor thing," she said. She hurried to free it, and as soon as she parted the branches the bird lifted its gleaming golden wings and flew out of the bush.

"You will have what you wish for," it sang to her, and the queen hurried back to the castle, full of joy.

And it was true. Before the year was over she had given birth to a baby daughter.

"I'd like to call her Briar Rose, after the bush in the garden," she said.

Well, the king thought it was a strange name to call a child, but he was so happy that he agreed. "We must have a great christening feast for her."

And the queen said, "She's a magic child, remember. I think we should invite the fairies."

So the invitations were sent out to all the fairies in the kingdom, but by mistake one of them was left out. It was a terrible mistake. Of all the fairies she was the most powerful. She was known as the Fairy of Shadows. She was a weaver of wicked spells.

On the day of the christening the air in the castle shimmered as if it was lit by stars, and a strange and wonderful humming came from nowhere, and then all of a sudden the hall was full of fairies, all bringing gifts for the baby Princess Briar Rose: bells for her music, flowers for her beauty, crystal water for her dancing – those sort of presents, fairy presents. The last fairy of all was just about to lay her gift in the cradle when there came a rushing of icy wind. All the candles flickered and the curtains floated like the waves of the sea. The air went cold and still. And there was the Fairy of Shadows, her eyes glowing like rubies in her white face. She stared at every one of them in turn, and nobody moved.

"Why was I not invited to the christening?" she demanded.

The king and queen rushed forward, begging forgiveness, but she swept past them as if they were invisible. She walked straight to the cradle where the baby Briar Rose lay fast asleep.

"I was not invited," said the Fairy of Shadows, "but all the same I have brought a gift."

From inside her cloak she drew a wreath of black flowers and tossed it on to the cradle. "This is my gift," she hissed. "On your fifteenth birthday you will prick your finger on the spindle of a spinning wheel. And you will die." And with that, the wicked

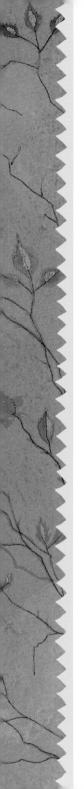

fairy swirled her black cloaks around herself in a cloud of rippling thunder, and she disappeared.

The king and queen wrung their hands in despair. "Can't you do something?" they begged.

But the fairies shook their heads and looked away. "She is the most powerful fairy of all. Nothing can undo her magic," they said.

And then the youngest fairy

stepped forward. "Wait," she said. "I haven't given my gift to the princess yet. It's true, I can't undo the magic of the Fairy of Shadows. But I can weaken it. Princess Briar Rose will prick her finger on her fifteenth birthday. But she won't die. Instead she will sleep for a hundred years. You will all sleep with her, every creature in this castle. She can only be wakened with a kiss. That is all I can do."

And the fairies turned into specks of golden pollen and blew away.

The queen lifted her baby out of the cradle and hugged her close. "What kind of a future is that?" she wept. "To sleep for a hundred years!"

The king put his arms round his wife and begged her to stop crying and to listen to him. "It would be a terrible thing, but it won't happen," he promised her. "I will order every spinning wheel in the country to be brought to the castle and burnt. It's so simple."

And that was exactly what he did. A huge bonfire was lit outside the castle and all the spinning wheels in the country were brought out and flung into it. Everybody was eager to help.

"Save the princess!" they sang.
"Let the wicked fairy do her worst;
We'll burn away her evil curse!"

But the wicked fairy watched from the shadows and laughed to herself.

Briar Rose had everything that the fairies wished for her; she was beautiful and clever, strong and healthy, wise and good. She could dance like a dragonfly and sing like a skylark, and what was more, everybody loved her. Her fifteenth birthday came, and her parents decided to hold a big party to celebrate it.

"And we've invited all the young princes," they told her. "They all want to meet you, Briar Rose."

"What for?"

"Why, to marry you, of course. One of those handsome princes may choose you to be his bride."

"Marry me! I don't want to get married! I don't want to meet any horrible handsome princes," Briar Rose said. "I just want to play with my friends in the castle."

But it was too late. They could hear the jingling of the approaching carriages, and the fanfare of trumpets announcing the arrival of the young

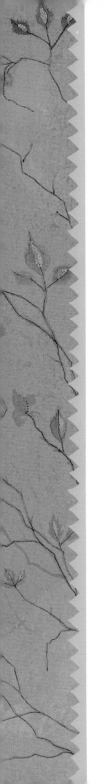

princes. The king and queen hurried to the great hall to get ready to welcome them, and Briar Rose decided that there was only one thing she could do to avoid the horrible handsome princes. She would have to hide. She ran out of the castle and into the gardens, and there she found a tower that she had never noticed before. She pushed open the door and stepped inside. She could hear the sound of something going *creak! creak! creak!* She climbed the shallow stairs to find out what was making the sound. There in the cobwebby attic she saw something she had never seen in her life before. It was a spinning wheel.

An old lady was spinning black strands of wool like the legs of giant spiders, and when she saw Briar Rose watching she didn't stop for a moment. She raised her hand in its black fingerless mitten and she said, "Would you like to try? Come here, my dear. Sit down beside me and I'll show you what to do."

Slowly, slowly, because she was a little bit afraid, Briar Rose approached the old woman and sat down beside her. The old woman smiled, and guided her hand, and as soon as Briar Rose touched the spindle she gave a gasp of pain, because it was as if the point had pierced her heart. Three drops of blood glistened on her finger. Instantly she fell asleep. The old woman swirled her black cloaks around her and disappeared.

The clock in the great hall of the castle stopped ticking. And the king and queen fell asleep; the serving-maid in the kitchen, the stable-lad and his horses, the butler and the parlour-maid, all yawned and slept. The chamber-maid fell into the bed she was making, the cook nodded into his cake bowl, the dogs curled up on the stairs, the cats and the mice lay down side by side, the candle flames fluttered and went out. The castle, and all its people, fell into a deep, deep sleep.

Around the castle there grew a forest that was so high and so deep that no light penetrated through. No birds flew there, no animals moved. Twined around every branch of every tree were briars, with thorns as sharp as needles. And so it remained for a hundred years.

News spread of the enchanted castle and the beautiful princess who slept inside it. Knights and princes came from all round the world and tried to fight their way through the trees to rescue her, but the forest was too thick and the thorns too sharp. They all died, every one, ripped to shreds. One day a young prince was walking near the forest and a golden bird flew over his head and dropped a feather. The prince bent to pick it up, and the feather turned into a key in his hand. "What can it be?" he asked. An old man was passing by, and he looked at the key and told the prince a story that his grandfather had told him, many years before. "Deep in that forest there's a castle, and by the castle is a tower. In the tower is a room, and in that room is a bed. And on that bed a princess lies. She's been there for a hundred years.

Not dead, young sir. Sleeping. That's the story I've heard. Go, sir, rescue her."

The old man went on his way, and the prince stood with the key in his hand not knowing what to do. Tattered rags fluttered from the branches of the forest trees, all that was left of the brave princes who had tried before him.

"I daren't go in there!" he said. "It's so dark and deep." Yet he thought of the princess who had lain under a spell for a hundred years, and who would never wake up unless she was rescued.

"I'll do it!" he said. "I'll try." He lifted up his sword to hack his way through, and instantly the golden bird flew down as if to show him the way. Roses grew on the briars, and the branches parted to let the sunlight through. The great trees swayed to let him pass, and there in the distance he could see the great castle with a tower standing near by. He went to the tower and climbed the stairs. He opened the door with his golden key, and there was the room, and there was the bed, and there was the princess lying on it, as fresh as if she had just fallen asleep that very minute.

"How beautiful she is!" the prince said, and without thinking he bent down and kissed her. And Princess Briar Rose opened her eyes.

The great clock in the castle started to tick. The king and queen yawned and stretched. The serving-maid in the kitchen, the stable-lad tending the horses, the butler, the parlour-maid, all rubbed their eyes. The chamber-maid jumped out of the bed and carried on making it, the cook jerked his head out of the cake bowl and licked his lips, the dogs strolled down the stairs, the cats chased the

mice, and the candle flames flickered back to life.

"You don't look as if you're over a hundred," the young prince said.

"A hundred!" Briar Rose laughed. "It's my fifteenth birthday!"

She stood up, and was so beautiful that the young prince fell on to his knees.

"Will you marry me?" he asked.

And Princess Briar Rose smiled at him and said *yes*.

TITLES IN THE FAIRY TALE SERIES

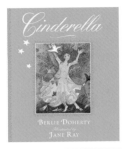

Cinderella

BERLIE DOHERTY
Illustrated by
JANE RAY

Beauty and the Beast

BERLIE DOHERTY
Illustrated by
JANE RAY

Aladdin

BERLIE DOHERTY
Illustrated by
JANE RAY

The Frog Prince

BERLIE DOHERTY
Illustrated by
JANE RAY

Rumpelstiltskin

BERLIE DOHERTY
Illustrated by
JANE RAY

Snow White

BERLIE DOHERTY
Illustrated by
JANE RAY

The Wild Swans

BERLIE DOHERTY
Illustrated by
JANE RAY

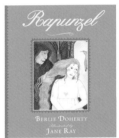

Rapunzel

BERLIE DOHERTY
Illustrated by
JANE RAY

Sleeping Beauty

BERLIE DOHERTY
Illustrated by
JANE RAY

Hansel and Gretel

BERLIE DOHERTY
Illustrated by
JANE RAY

Available from all good bookstores

www.walker.co.uk

FOR THE BEST CHILDREN'S BOOKS, LOOK FOR THE BEAR.